RUBY JOINS THE CHOIR

WRITTEN BY:
R.K. BARRETT

THIS BOOK BELONGS TO:

_____

ILLUSTRATED BY:
ANA CHAVEZ

This book is dedicated to my precious daughters,

Maddisan and Amira.

In loving memory of my maternal grandmother

Della C.Harmon.

Her singing legacy lives on!

Early one Sunday morning, Ruby and Grammy got dressed in their fancy hats and dresses and drove to church. Ruby was very excited and happily hummed during the entire ride.

As they approached the church doors, Ruby could hear loud voices singing beautifully. When the doors opened, Ruby realized it was the church choir creating the sweet melody.

2

Ruby sat through church daydreaming and imagining herself singing on stage. "What if that was me singing with the choir?" she thought. Ruby could hardly wait for church to end so she could tell Grammy how much she enjoyed listening to the choir.

3

"Grammy, Grammy! How can I sing like the choir?"

"Ruby, honey, I'm a bit tired. Let's talk when we get home and you have changed out of your dress," Grammy replied.

Excited, Ruby rushed into her room when they arrived at the house. She quickly changed out of her Sunday outfit and into her pajamas.

Ruby ran into the living room and found Grammy sitting in her favorite rocking chair. "What is it child? What has gotten you so worked up and excited?" Grammy asked.

Ruby looked up at Grammy with a huge smile and asked,"Did you hear the choir today at church? Did you see the way they swayed?"
"Why yes," Grammy replied while smiling. "The choir sang beautifully today."

Ruby began to jump up and down with glee. She looked up at Grammy and said, "I want to join the choir Grammy! Can I please?" "Oh Ruby! That would be great! Are you sure that you would like to sing with the choir at church?" she asked.

Ruby grabbed Grammy by the hands and pulled her off her rocking chair. They joyfully laughed and spun around the room like a carousel as Ruby sang, "I do! I do! I do!"

"But," Grammy said with her finger in the air.
"Ruby, we have a few steps to take before joining the choir."
"What do we need to do Grammy?" asked Ruby.

"First, we must let Mrs. Horn know you would like to join the choir. She is the lady that plays the piano. We can meet her on Wednesday night when the choir has practice."

That night Ruby sang herself to sleep. She was anxious for Wednesday to come. She knew that she would do well because she had always sung for family and friends.

The next morning Ruby sang as she got ready for school...

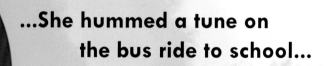

...She hummed a tune on the bus ride to school...

...And she daydreamed about singing in the choir during class...

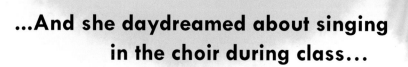

During the bus ride home, the bus driver could hear Ruby humming. He told her that she had a very nice voice. Ruby thanked him and told him that she was going to sing in her church choir. "I know you will do great Ruby," he shouted as drove off.

Later that night after dinner, Grammy heard Ruby singing in the bathtub. Ruby was singing one of her favorite songs while imagining herself on a big stage with bubbles everywhere.

Tuesday morning, Ruby woke up ready to take on the day. She sang and sang and sang all day long. When she got home, she hurried to eat her dinner and skipped off to bed.

"Why are you moving so fast child?" Grammy asked.
"Grammy, if I hurry and get to bed, it will be Wednesday soon, and you know what that means!" Ruby replied.
Grammy smiled and confirmed,"yes Ruby, I do. Well good night then kiddo."

Finally, it was Wednesday morning and Ruby jumped out of bed to get ready for school. She spent the whole day practicing the song she wanted to sing for Mrs. Horn.

She practiced while feeding the fish...

She practiced during recess...

Ruby practiced while watering
the classroom garden...

18

That afternoon, Ruby burst through the front door of her house. Ruby dropped her bookbag on the floor, and ran into Grammy's room shouting,"Grammy! Grammy! IT'S TIME TO PRACTICE WITH THE CHOIR!". At 5 o'clock, they jumped into Grammy's bright red car and sang a joyful song all the way to church.

When Ruby walked into the church, everyone was excited to see the young girl who was eager to join their choir. Mrs. Horn welcomed Ruby and asked her to sing a short song.

For the first time ever, Ruby felt nervous to sing. She didn't know why she felt that way. Ruby looked around at all the smiling faces expecting her to sing. Her eyes were wide open, and she felt sweat beads forming on her forehead. She opened her mouth to sing, but nothing would come out!

21

Grammy took Ruby by the hand and began to slowly sing the song they had been singing in the car:

"I am who I am, and I can be anything,
with You, Oh Lord, you guide me..."

Ruby joined in with a shy shaky voice.

"Oh Lord please lead me, guide me through."

Mrs. Horn began to play the melody for the song on the piano.

Ruby's voice began to get stronger, and the choir joined in singing softly in the background.

Suddenly, Ruby belted out with a strong beautiful voice. Her voice was so sweet that it amazed the choir and they stopped singing! Everyone began to clap for Ruby. Grammy was so proud of Ruby.

She hugged her and whispered in her ear, "Great job Sweetheart! Remember whenever you feel shy to just open your heart and sing!"

Ruby gleefully practiced during the rest of the week.

She sang while painting Fluffy's nails...

She practiced while
Grammy did her hair...

And she hummed while she
washed the dishes after dinner...

25

On Sunday, Ruby joined the choir on stage. Before she sang her song, she remembered what Grammy said. She opened her heart and sang so beautifully that everyone in the audience stood up and applauded.

After church, everyone greeted Ruby and told her what an amazing job she had done. Ruby was so happy that she could not wait until next Sunday to sing with the choir again!

During the car ride home from church, Ruby smiled with glee. Grammy looked in her rearview mirror and said, "You see Ruby, with practice and a bit of courage, you can do anything you put your mind to."

"Yes, Grammy!" Ruby, gasps and shouts. "Up next, I will join the school play!" Grammy and Ruby laughed as they rode off into the sunset.

I AM LYRICS

By R.K. Barrett

I am who I am and I can be anything
With you , oh Lord, you guide me
You give me favor
And I have faith in you
O Lord please lead me and guide me through.

I can do all things through Christ who strengthens
me when the world
Says I can't you're always there for me
When I am down you always comfort me
I just lift my head up high and believe

Chorus
I am who I am and I can be anything
With you , oh Lord, you guide me
You give me favor
And I have faith in you
O Lord please lead me and guide me through.

I know that life it can be confusing at times
You have so many questions and not enough
answers for whats inside
I can see it in your eyes
And sometimes you wanna cry
But theres a greater strength in you , have to push
through, hold your head up high and say......

Chorus
I am who I am and I can be anything
With you , oh Lord, you guide me
You give me favor
And I have faith in you
O Lord please lead me and guide me through.

Bridge...
I can do anything
I can do anything
I can!
(repeat)

I can do anything (ohhh ohh I know I can)
I can do anything (ohh ohh I know I can)
I can!

I am who I am and I can be anything
With you , oh Lord, you guide me....(fade out)